To my magical daughter, my golden niece
and all the kids reading this book.

Remember to always follow your heart.
It leads to your rainbow!

Once there was a unicorn with a
golden heart named Kara.

The unicorn truly believed that we all
have good golden hearts.

Kara said,

"I want to follow my heart and go on the journey
that leads me to my very own rainbow."

So she set off on a magical adventure.

Kara saw her mum and dad near the stream by their forest home. They asked her,

"Where are you going Kara?"

She bravely said,

"I want to follow my heart and go on the journey
that leads me to my rainbow."

Kara's mum and dad celebrated when they heard she wanted to find her rainbow and cheered her on her way.

She hugged them both goodbye and started her exciting adventure.

On the journey, Kara walked past a grumpy looking bear.

His golden heart was pale and not as bright as Kara's golden heart.

The grumpy bear asked her,

"Where are you going little unicorn?"

She bravely said,

"I am following my heart and going on the journey that will lead me to my rainbow."

The grumpy bear said,

"I don't think you will find your rainbow."

Kara noticed the grumpy bear had a thorn in his paw. He was in pain. This was why his golden heart was paler than the unicorn's.

She helped him pull the thorn out. Now
his golden heart shone brightly.

The now, not so grumpy bear, thanked
Kara and cheered her on her way.

She waved goodbye and
continued her adventure.

On the journey, Kara saw a scary looking bridge. Kara was not sure if she should cross the scary looking bridge...

but then she saw her brightly coloured
rainbow sparkling on the other side.

She bravely said,

"I will follow my heart and complete the
journey that leads me to my rainbow."

Kara crossed the bridge.

She made it safely to the other side and was very happy to find her rainbow there.

The little unicorn touched her rainbow...

and her golden heart started
to glow even brighter.

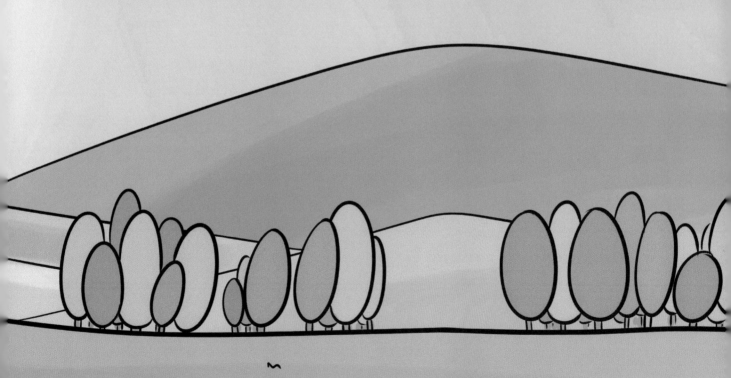

Printed in Great Britain
by Amazon

17626432R00016